Cambridge Early Years

Communication and Language

for English as a First Language

Learner's Book 3B

Gill Budgell

Contents

Note to parents and practitioners 3

Block 3: Caring for ourselves and the world 4

Block 4: Then and now 19

Acknowledgements 32

Note to parents and practitioners

This Learner's Book provides activities to support the second term of FLE Communication and Language for Cambridge Early Years 3.

Activities can be used at school or at home. Children will need support from an adult. Additional guidance about activities can be found in the **For practitioners** boxes.

Stories are provided for children to enjoy looking at and listening to. Children are not expected to be able to read the stories themselves.

Children will encounter the following characters within this book. You could ask children to point to the characters when they see them on the pages, and say their names.

The Learner's Book activities support the Teaching Resource activities. The Teaching Resource provides step-by-step coverage of the Cambridge Early Years curriculum and guidance on how the Learner's Book activities develop the curriculum learning statements.

Hi, my name is Mia.

Find us on the front covers doing lots of fun activities.

Hi, my name is Gemi.

Hi, my name is Rafi.

Hi, my name is Kiho.

Block 3 — Caring for ourselves and the world

Bloom by Anne Booth

There once was a beautiful flower which grew under the window of a big house, and a little girl who loved it.

Every morning, on her way to school with her brother, the little girl would visit the flower.

She would look at its beautiful petals, drink in its sweet smell, and wonder at the smoothness of its leaves and at their colour and shape.

'Good morning, beautiful flower,' she would say. 'I think you're wonderful. Thank you for being here for us. I love you,' and she would go to school happy.

One morning, the man living in the big house woke up early and heard someone talking to his flower. He looked out of his window and saw the little girl.

'How dare you talk to MY flower?' he shouted. 'Go away and never come near my flower again!'

The little girl and her brother didn't like being shouted at, so they went to school another way.

The next day, when the
sun rose, the flower did not open.
And every day after that it stayed tight shut.
The man was furious and sent for his gardener.

'What is the matter with my flower?' he demanded.
'Is it getting enough water?'

'Yes,' said the gardener. 'I water it every morning and evening.'

'Well, you're obviously not doing it properly,' said the man crossly.
'I can see that I am just going to have to do it for myself.'

And so every morning he got up and watered the flower,
and every evening before he went to bed he watered the flower.
But it still refused to open.

'Maybe it needs more shade?' said the man.
'The sun is very hot in the middle of the day.'

'I have made sure it has plenty of shade,' said the gardener.

But the man said, **'well, you're obviously not doing it properly. I can see I am just going to have to do it myself.'**

So every day, when the sun was at its highest, he took his umbrella and shaded the flower from the heat. But it still didn't open.

He watered the flower in the morning and shaded from the midday sun

and watered it again just before he went to bed.

The man began to talk to it. He told it how wonderful he was,

how lucky it was to be his flower, and how important his job was.

But it still didn't open.

He told it all about his problems, how busy he was, and the fact that nobody liked him.

He complained about how his gardener was rubbish, how if he didn't do everything, nothing got done properly, and how lonely he felt.

He ordered it to bloom for him to cheer him up.

The unhappy man called the gardener to him again.

'Before you say ANYTHING,' said the gardener, 'I don't know what the matter is. All I know is that the flower hasn't opened since you sent away the little school girl who passed by it every morning.'

'**What did she do that I don't do?**' said the man crossly.

'Well, she used to talk to it every day,' said the gardener.

'**That can't be it,**' said the man. 'I talk to it every morning, at midday and before I go to bed, and what I can say must be MUCH better than anything a little girl could say.'

The man thought and thought.

'I can see I am just going to have to ask that child to come back. Maybe she has some magic words which make the flower bloom.'

So he went to the school gate and waited for the little girl and her brother to arrive.

'My flower stopped blooming after you left,' said the man to the little girl.

'Poor flower,' said the little girl.

'I've watered it and sheltered it and talked to it every day, but still it won't open,' and a tear rolled down his cheek.

'What do you say to it?' said the little girl, and her brother passed the man a hankie.

'Well,' said the man, blowing his nose. 'I tell it how important I am and how lucky it is to be in my garden. I tell it how miserable I am. I tell it how horrible everybody else is, and I order it to bloom to cheer me up. But it doesn't work.'

'Well,' said the little girl. 'Why don't you tell it how wonderful it is, thank it for being there, and how much you love it? That's what I always did.'

So the man ran home to his flower and said **'You are wonderful.'** And as he said the words, he realised for the first time how truly wonderful the flower was.

'I'm so lucky you grow in my garden,' he said, and as he said it he realised how truly lucky he was, and how he hadn't ever really looked at his flower properly, and how much he longed to see it and smell its perfume again.

'I love you so much,' said the man at last, and as he said it, his own heart filled with love.

And the flower bloomed.

Who says it?

Match and say.

Match each character to the correct speech bubble. Say it like they would.

My flower stopped blooming after you left.

I water it every morning and evening.

Good morning, beautiful flower.

For practitioners
Children draw a line with a pencil or their finger to match the characters to the correct speech bubble. Refer back to the story as needed to remind them of the characters and what they say. Encourage them to repeat the sentences, speaking like the characters do.

A flower in bloom

Create.

Use materials to complete the flower picture.

For practitioners
Encourage children to think about what they can use to make a beautiful flower. They may need collage materials and glue. Ask children to have a go at naming basic parts of the plant and write them if they wish.

My flower of wonderful things

Draw and say.

Think of something wonderful to draw in each petal.

For practitioners

Remind children of any similar activities in class and encourage them to think, draw and say what they think is wonderful. The children draw inside each petal and some may want to try to write labels too. Support as necessary.

Tree by Jenny Boult

bird home
leaf home
ant home
lizard home
twig
branch
caterpillar home

seed shade
sheep shade
cow shade
horse shade
wallaby shade
people shade
ground shade
sun shade

a tree is a green umbrella
with brown bits

Trees and shade

Sort and say.

Circle things you can find in a tree. Draw a square around the things that like shade from the tree.

For practitioners

Children circle the things that can be found in trees (*bird, leaf, ant, lizard, twig, branch, caterpillar*). Then ask them to draw a square around the things that enjoy shade from the tree (*seed, sheep, cow, horse, wallaby, people*). Refer back to the poem as needed.

Block 4 Then and now

Big Bugs by Claire Llewellyn

CONTENTS

A giant bug	2
Goliath beetle	3
Atlas moth	4
Stick insect	5
Tarantula spider	6
Giant dragonfly	8
Big bug chart	8

A giant bug

Most bugs are very small but some of them are GIANTS! This is a giant water bug. It lives in ponds and lakes. It can swim well but it can also fly.

HOW BIG?

See how big each bug is next to a ruler. This giant water bug is 7 centimetres long.

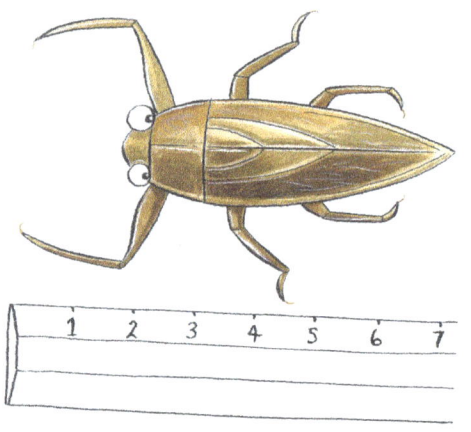

Goliath beetle

The Goliath **beetle** is the biggest beetle in the world.
It is very heavy too.
It lives in the rainforests in Africa.
The Goliath beetle feeds on plants.
It eats the sweet **sap** that drips from trees.

HOW BIG?
A Goliath beetle can be 12 centimetres long.

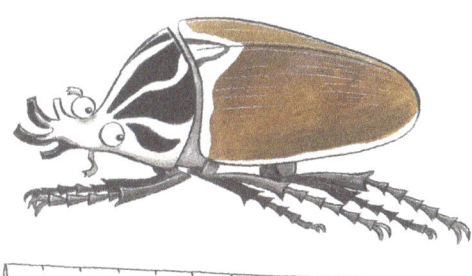

BUG FACTS
Beetles have wings and can fly.

Wings

Legs

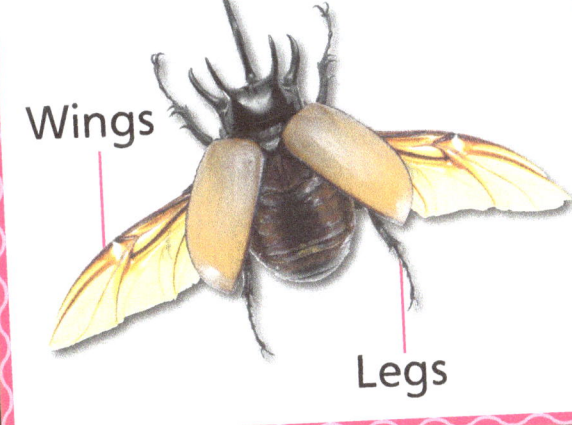

Atlas moth

This is the world's largest moth. It lives in warm, wet places. This moth lives in the **rainforests** of India.

BUG FACTS

A male moth has big **antennae** on its head. The antennae help it to pick up smells in the air.

Antennae
Body
Wings

HOW BIG?

The **wingspan** of this Atlas moth is 25–27 centimetres wide.

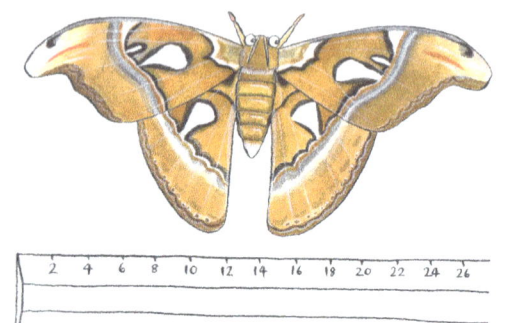

Stick insect

The world's longest **insect** lives in the trees.
Its body looks just like a stick.
This helps to hide it from hungry birds.

Can you see a stick insect in this tree?

HOW BIG?
The largest stick insects are over 50 centimetres long.

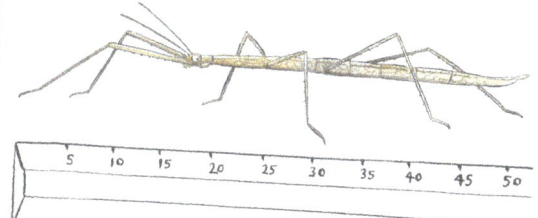

BUG FACTS
All insects have six legs.
Antennae
Legs

Tarantula spider

Tarantulas are the biggest spiders on Earth.

They live in rainforests in South America.

Tarantulas rest in the day.

At night they hunt for beetles, frogs and other small animals.

HOW BIG?
A tarantula spider's leg span can be 30 centimetres wide.

BUG FACTS
Tarantulas have eight long, hairy legs.

Hairs

Legs

Giant dragonfly

This brown and yellow giant is a dragonfly.
It lives near muddy **bogs**.
It flies over the bog and looks for food.

HOW BIG?

This dragonfly's body is 12 centimetres long. Its **wingspan** can be 14 centimetres wide.

BUG FACTS

Dragonflies can see very well. They have huge **compound eyes**. They can spot flies and other insects.

Eyes

Big bug chart

	a giant bug	Goliath beetle	Atlas moth	stick insect	tarantula spider	giant dragonfly
Lives in water	✓					
Lives in trees		✓	✓	✓	✓	
Lives by bogs						✓
Feeds on plants		✓		✓		
Feeds on animals	✓				✓	✓
Has wings	✓	✓	✓			✓
Has antennae	✓	✓	✓	✓		✓
Has six legs	✓	✓	✓	✓		✓
Has eight legs					✓	

There are six bugs in this book. Where do most of them like to live?

Glossary

Antenna: part on a bug's head that help it to feel, smell and taste
Beetle: insect that has hard covers over its soft wings
Bog: very wet land
Compound eyes: eyes that are made up of many little parts
Insect: small animal with three parts to its body and six legs
Rainforest: forest that grows in very warm, wet places
Sap: sweet liquid that comes from plants
Wingspan: how wide an animal is across its wings

Bug book cover

Trace and write.

Write the title on the book.
Draw a big bug on the front cover.

Big Bugs

For practitioners
Encourage children to use their phonics as appropriate to read the tracing letters of the book title *Big Bugs*. Ask them to trace with a finger before using a pencil to write the letters. Encourage them to choose a big bug to draw on the cover.

Which bug am I?

Match and say.

Match each speech bubble to the correct bug.

I look like a stick. ●　　　●

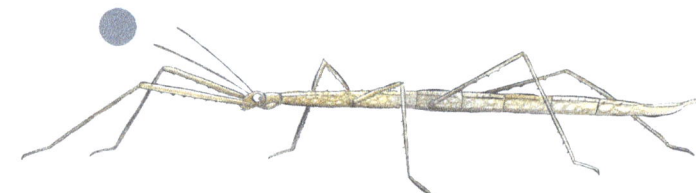

My eight legs are hairy. ●　　　●

I am the biggest moth in the world. ●　　　●

I am the biggest beetle in the world.   •   •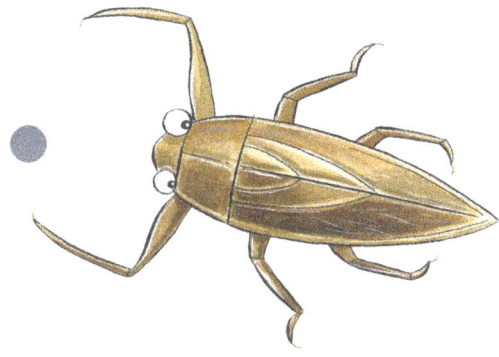

I have very big eyes.   •   •

I live in water.   •   •

For practitioners
Support children to read and understand the speech bubbles, and to draw a line to match each statement to the correct bug. Refer to the text if helpful.

Busy Bugs
by James Carter

Out in the garden
look down low
see all the busy bugs
come and go …

tiny bugs
that feed on leaves

merry bugs
that buzz all day

shiny bugs
that creep up trees

scaredy bugs
that whizz away

fancy bugs
that chirp in grass

wiggly bugs
that hide in sand

bouncy bugs
that leap so fast
Out in the garden …

tickly bugs
that like your hand

Out in the garden
look down low
see all the busy bugs
come and go …

Tickly bugs

Draw and say.

Draw around your hand. Add some tickly bugs.

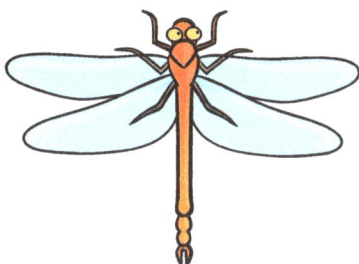

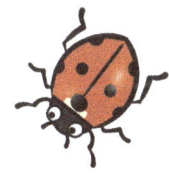

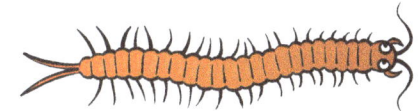

For practitioners

Support children to draw around their hand, noting if they are right- or left-handed. Talk about the bugs and which ones they think might be tickly on their hand. Children can draw bugs onto their hand image, or create them with collage materials and stick them on with glue.

Acknowledgements

The authors and publishers acknowledge the following sources of copyright material and are grateful for the permissions granted. While every effort has been made, it has not always been possible to identify the sources of all the material used, or to trace all copyright holders. If any omissions are brought to our notice, we will be happy to include the appropriate acknowledgements on reprinting.

BLOOM by Anne Booth and Robyn Wilson-Owen First published in the UK by Tiny Owl Publishing Ltd 2020 Text Copyright © Anne Booth 2020 Illustrations Copyright © Robyn Wilson-Owen 2020

'Tree' by Jenny Boult appeared in *The Green Umbrella* ed. Jill Brand, A&C Black

Big Bugs by Claire Llewellyn, Cambridge Reading Adventures © 2016 Cambridge University Press and UCL Institute of Education (Photo credits: (Goliath beetle and bird-eating spider) Piotr Naskrecki/Minden Pictures/FLPA; (giant water bug) Hector Ruiz Villar/Shutterstock; (inset beetle) bluehand/Shutterstock; (Atlas moth) gracious_tiger/Shutterstock; (inset moth) aodaodaodaod/Shutterstock; (stick insect) SANIREN/Shutterstock; (inset stick insect) Melinda Fawver/Shutterstock; (inset tarantula) Olgysha/Shutterstock; (dragonfly) Ken Griffiths, NHPA/Photoshot; (inset dragonfly) Hintu Aliaksei/Shutterstock)

'Busy bugs' from *A Ticket to Kalamazoo!* by James Carter, illustrated by Neal Layton, Otter-Barry Books. Used by permission of the publisher.

Thanks to the following artist at Beehive Illustration:

Jo Litchfield.

Cover characters by Becky Davies (The Bright Agency)